Dear Parents:

Congratulations! Your child is taking the first steps on an exciting journey. The destination? Independent reading!

STEP INTO READING® will help your child get there. The program offers five steps to reading success. Each step includes fun stories and colorful art or photographs. In addition to original fiction and books with favorite characters, there are Step into Reading Non-Fiction Readers, Phonics Readers and Boxed Sets, Sticker Readers, and Comic Readers—a complete literacy program with something to interest every child.

Learning to Read, Step by Step!

Ready to Read   Preschool–Kindergarten
• big type and easy words • rhyme and rhythm • picture clues
For children who know the alphabet and are eager to begin reading.

Reading with Help   Preschool–Grade 1
• basic vocabulary • short sentences • simple stories
For children who recognize familiar words and sound out new words with help.

Reading on Your Own   Grades 1–3
• engaging characters • easy-to-follow plots • popular topics
For children who are ready to read on their own.

Reading Paragraphs   Grades 2–3
• challenging vocabulary • short paragraphs • exciting stories
For newly independent readers who read simple sentences with confidence.

Ready for Chapters   Grades 2–4
• chapters • longer paragraphs • full-color art
For children who want to take the plunge into chapter books but still like colorful pictures.

STEP INTO READING® is designed to give every child a successful reading experience. The grade levels are only guides; children will progress through the steps at their own speed, developing confidence in their reading.

Remember, a lifetime love of reading starts with a single step!

Step into Reading, Random House, and the Random House colophon are registered trademarks of Penguin Random House LLC.

Visit us on the Web!
StepIntoReading.com
rhcbooks.com

Educators and librarians, for a variety of teaching tools, visit us at RHTeachersLibrarians.com

ISBN 978-0-525-64761-4 (trade) — ISBN 978-0-525-64762-1 (lib. bdg.)
ISBN 978-0-525-64763-8 (ebook)

Printed in the United States of America
10 9 8 7 6 5 4 3 2 1

DREAMWORKS

TROLLS

Color Day Party!

by Mary Man-Kong
illustrated by Fabio Laguna

Random House 🏠 New York

It is a busy day
in Troll Village.
Everyone is getting ready
for the Color Day party.
All the Trolls will wear
their favorite color.

There are so many
great colors!
Poppy does not know
which color to wear.

She decides to ask
her friends.

In Troll Village,
Poppy meets Cooper.
Cooper is going
to wear red.
He has an idea.

He gives Poppy
a red scarf.
Poppy loves red.
Maybe she will wear
red, too!

DJ Suki is going
to wear orange.
"I am rocking the orange,"
she says.

She gives Poppy
orange headphones.
Poppy loves orange.
Maybe she will wear
orange, too!

11

Smidge is going
to wear yellow.
"Yellow gives
me strength,"
she says.

She gives Poppy
a yellow bow.
Poppy loves yellow.
Maybe she will wear
yellow, too!

Fuzzbert is tickled
to be green.
His fuzzy hair
tickles Poppy!
Fuzzbert has an idea.

He gives Poppy
a green bracelet.
Poppy loves green.
Maybe she will wear
green, too!

Even Branch is going
to wear his favorite color.
He will wear blue.

He gives Poppy
a blue vest.
Poppy loves blue.
Maybe she will wear
blue, too!

Poppy visits
Satin and Chenille.
They are going
to wear indigo
and violet.

They give her
an indigo jumper
and violet leggings.
Poppy loves those colors.
Maybe she will wear
them, too!

When Poppy gets home,
she does not know
what to do.

She loves all
the different colors.
Suddenly,
Poppy has an idea.

At the Color Day party,
everyone wears
a different color.

But Poppy wears
all the colors!

She looks like a rainbow.

The Trolls love it!

Happy
Color Day!

Dear Parents:

Congratulations! Your child is taking the first steps on an exciting journey. The destination? Independent reading!

STEP INTO READING® will help your child get there. The program offers five steps to reading success. Each step includes fun stories and colorful art or photographs. In addition to original fiction and books with favorite characters, there are Step into Reading Non-Fiction Readers, Phonics Readers and Boxed Sets, Sticker Readers, and Comic Readers—a complete literacy program with something to interest every child.

Learning to Read, Step by Step!

Ready to Read   Preschool–Kindergarten
• big type and easy words • rhyme and rhythm • picture clues
For children who know the alphabet and are eager to begin reading.

Reading with Help   Preschool–Grade 1
• basic vocabulary • short sentences • simple stories
For children who recognize familiar words and sound out new words with help.

Reading on Your Own   Grades 1–3
• engaging characters • easy-to-follow plots • popular topics
For children who are ready to read on their own.

Reading Paragraphs   Grades 2–3
• challenging vocabulary • short paragraphs • exciting stories
For newly independent readers who read simple sentences with confidence.

Ready for Chapters   Grades 2–4
• chapters • longer paragraphs • full-color art
For children who want to take the plunge into chapter books but still like colorful pictures.

STEP INTO READING® is designed to give every child a successful reading experience. The grade levels are only guides; children will progress through the steps at their own speed, developing confidence in their reading.

Remember, a lifetime love of reading starts with a single step!

Step into Reading, Random House, and the Random House colophon are registered trademarks of Penguin Random House LLC.

Visit us on the Web!
StepIntoReading.com
rhcbooks.com

Educators and librarians, for a variety of teaching tools, visit us at RHTeachersLibrarians.com

ISBN 978-0-525-64761-4 (trade) — ISBN 978-0-525-64762-1 (lib. bdg.)
ISBN 978-0-525-64763-8 (ebook)

Printed in the United States of America
10 9 8 7 6 5 4 3 2 1

DREAMWORKS

Trolls

The Sound of Spring

by David Lewman

illustrated by Fabio Laguna

Random House New York

It is a warm spring night
in Troll Village.
All the Trolls are sleeping,
except one.

Branch is wide awake.

He hears something.

What's that sound?

It sounds like chirping.
Is there a bird
in the house?

Branch looks around.

No bird!

In the morning,
Branch still hears
chirping.

He checks the village.
He cannot find
what is making
the sound.

The chirping is
driving him crazy!

Branch asks Cloud Guy
if he hears the sound.
Cloud Guy listens.

He hears
the chirping, too.
He asks Branch
if *he* is making the sound.

Branch says no.
Cloud Guy says
Branch *must*
be chirping!

Branch says,
"I am *not* chirping!"
Branch thinks Cloud Guy
is playing a trick on him.

He is angry.

He chases Cloud Guy

through the woods!

Poppy sees her friends.
She asks them
what's wrong.
Branch tells Poppy
about the chirping.

Poppy listens closely.
She knows where
the sound
is coming from!

Poppy reaches into
Branch's hair
and pulls out an egg!

That is where
the chirping
is coming from!
A bird must have laid
an egg in Branch's hair!

Poppy says the egg
is about to hatch!

A bird comes out
of the egg.
It sings a song.
Poppy and Branch
sing, too!

The little bird's
mother hears
her baby singing.
She comes right away!

They fly off together.

Everyone waves goodbye.
Branch misses the bird's
chirping a little . . .
but not *too* much.